MARK ANTHONY BROWN

THE EASTER EGG HUNT

Copyright @ Mark Anthony Brown 2024
Mark Anthony Brown asserts the moral right to be identified as the author of this work

All Rights Reserved.
This novel is entirely a work of fiction.
The names, characters and incidents portrayed in it are the work of the author's imagination. Any resemblance to actual persons, living or dead, events or localities is entirely coincidental.

All rights reserved. No part of this publication may be reproduced, stored in a retrieval system, or transmitted, in any form or by any means, electronic, mechanical, photocopying, recording or otherwise, without the prior permission of the publisher.

Prologue

Long ago, before the streets of Maplewood had seen the steady march of time, it was a small, quiet town nestled between the rolling hills, where the air was always crisp, the trees always full of songbirds, and the people were as warm and welcoming as the hearths in their homes. Maplewood, known for its gentle beauty and its sleepy charm, was a place where everyone knew everyone, and nothing ever seemed out of place.

Yet, even in the most peaceful of places, there are whispers - whispers about things that cannot always be explained, about events that happen without warning or reason. And so it was that one bright spring morning, just as the town was preparing for its annual Easter Egg Hunt, a figure arrived. A stranger.

Clad in a long, dark coat and a wide-brimmed hat that shaded his face, he seemed to materialise from the very mist of the morning, as though the air itself had whispered him into existence. He spoke to no one, and no one spoke to him. He simply moved through the town with a quiet determination, leaving behind no more than a lingering shadow in his wake. He was not rude, nor unfriendly - he was simply... there. And he would not leave until his work was done.

On the morning of the Easter Egg Hunt, as the children scrambled in excited anticipation, the stranger began to hide eggs. But these were no ordinary eggs. For within the delicate shells, there lay something far more remarkable than candy or sweets. There lay a reflection of the heart itself.

The eggs were painted in all manner of ways - some dazzling, some plain, some intricate, others simple - but they were more than just decorations. They were something deeper, something the children could not yet understand. Each egg was a mirror, a mirror of the soul, showing not what a person seemed to be on the outside, but what they truly were on the inside.

For in the town of Maplewood, there were children who were kind and generous, who shared and cared without hesitation. And there were children who were vain, selfish, and spoiled, who thought only of themselves and what they could gain. The stranger knew, as he watched them with his knowing eyes, that the eggs would reveal a truth - one that would not be easily forgotten.

But that truth would not come without cost. The Easter Egg Hunt, in all its joy and anticipation, would be a test. A test of character, of kindness, of self-awareness. And only those who could see beyond the surface, who could look into their hearts and find the good within, would uncover the true treasures hidden inside the eggs.

The story of the stranger, and the lesson he would leave behind, would change Maplewood forever. The town would never again be the same. And from that moment forward, every year, as Easter approached and the children prepared for the hunt, they would remember the lesson the stranger had taught them - that true beauty, true value, lies not in what the eye can see, but in what the heart holds.

But for now, the eggs waited, hidden all over Maplewood, ready to be discovered.

And so, the hunt began.

CHAPTER ONE

The Stranger's Arrival

The morning sun stretched its golden fingers across the quiet town of Maplewood, a sleepy village that sat nestled among fields and woods, where life moved at its own deliberate pace. In the town square, the shops were just beginning to open, their owners sweeping the front steps and preparing for another Easter weekend - an event everyone eagerly anticipated. Children had already begun to chatter with excitement, their thoughts firmly fixed on the Easter Egg Hunt, which was only two days away.

It was a peaceful day, the kind where everything felt a little more vibrant, a little more alive with the promise of spring. Birds trilled in the trees, flowers bloomed along the cobbled streets, and the scent of freshly baked pastries wafted from Mrs. Pendle's bakery. The town had not yet caught wind of the unusual arrival that would soon change the course of their Easter celebrations.

He appeared out of nowhere, as strangers often do.

The man wore a long, dark coat that swirled about his ankles as he strode through the town's streets with a strange, measured gait. His wide-brimmed hat shadowed his face, hiding his features from the townsfolk who, as a rule, were always quick to take notice of new faces.

It was not his clothes, nor his walk, that turned heads - though both were peculiar enough - but the air of quiet mystery that clung to him like a second skin. He did not stop to speak to anyone. Not to the greengrocer who was setting out baskets of bright yellow daffodils. Not to the old women gossiping at the corner of Whittaker's Pub. Not even to the children who dashed past him, their laughter echoing in the crisp morning air.

The man simply walked, his footsteps soft and deliberate, as if he had a destination only he knew.

In his right hand, he carried a large wicker basket, and every now and then, he would pause by a tree, a bench, or a low wall. With the care of a cat concealing a secret, he would gently place something in the grass or behind a shrub.

It was only after he had passed and the children came running out in search of adventure that anyone took notice.

'Look!' cried young Henry Pendle, a boy with a shock of red hair and a mischievous grin that was usually reserved for the pranks he played on his sisters. He pointed toward the far side of the square, where a large, elegant egg - glittering and painted in swirling colours - lay half-hidden beneath a bench.

Sophie Eastwick, a quiet girl with kind eyes and a generous heart, gasped and pointed in the opposite direction. 'And there! Another one!' she cried.

The children sprinted toward the eggs, their shoes tapping a staccato rhythm on the cobblestones. Some stumbled, tripping over with their excitement, while others, more cautious, circled the objects with awe before reaching down to pick them up.

Each egg was unique - finely decorated, glittering with delicate patterns, and shimmering in the sunlight like the perfect embodiment of Easter magic. Some were striped in shades of pink and gold, others adorned with tiny silver stars or roses painted in pastel hues. They were beautiful, almost too beautiful.

But as the children clutched their prize, there was something strange about them. The eggs felt oddly warm to the touch, as though they were alive. And yet, despite their perfection, a faint, lingering sense of unease seemed to hang in the air, unnoticed by the children, but felt by a few of the adults who observed them from the windows of the shops.

Sophie, breathless from the excitement, turned to Henry with wide eyes. 'Where did they come from?' she asked, her voice low with curiosity. 'I've never seen eggs like this before.'

Henry, clutching his own egg tightly, grinned. 'Does it matter? It's the Easter Hunt, Soph. Don't look a gift egg in the... well, you know.' His voice trailed off as he marvelled at the intricate patterns on the egg in his hands.

Sophie glanced about, as though waiting for someone to explain. 'I wonder if it's Mr. Whittaker's doing,' she mused aloud, the old man who ran the town's pub and always seemed to know more about everything than anyone else. 'He has a knack for strange surprises.'

But no one had seen Mr. Whittaker that morning.

Before Sophie could ask another question, the man in the dark coat appeared again, crossing the square with the same purposeful stride. His basket, now noticeably lighter, swayed gently in his hand. The children - those who had noticed him, anyway - stared at him with wide eyes, but he did not acknowledge them.

By the time the man had walked out of sight, the town square was alive with whispers.

'Did you see that?'

'What on earth was he doing?'

'Is it part of the Easter Hunt?'

But no one had the answers, not even Mrs. Pendle, who had spent the better part of her life baking hot cross buns for every family in town.

By noon, the man had vanished as suddenly as he had appeared, but the eggs remained - hidden carefully in bushes, tucked beneath fences, and lodged between the branches of trees. Each one more exquisite than the last, each one shimmering in the sunlight like a tiny treasure chest waiting to be opened.

The children were beside themselves with excitement. They spoke in hushed tones of their finds, comparing eggs and guessing what delights might be hidden within. Sophie felt a flutter of unease, though she couldn't quite place why. It was as though the eggs, so lovely on the outside, were somehow too perfect, as though they were waiting for something - or someone.

'What if... what if there are more?' Sophie whispered, her curiosity piqued. She turned to Henry, who was already off again, scanning the square for any hint of the next egg.

But no one could have predicted how quickly things would change.

As dusk fell, the town buzzed with the mystery of the day. There were no signs of the man, but his eggs had left a trail of wonder in their wake. No one could be sure if he would return, but every corner of Maplewood seemed to hold the promise of another hidden treasure.

And as the children tucked their new eggs away, they had no idea that this Easter would bring more than just an ordinary hunt - it would bring a lesson none of them would ever forget.

CHAPTER TWO

The Town Prepares

The sky over Maplewood was the colour of new butter - soft, golden, and warm - casting its gentle light over the town as preparations for the annual Easter Egg Hunt moved into full swing. It was the event of the year, a celebration that brought excitement to every home, whether through the baking of sugar cookies or the careful painting of egg shells. The sound of scurrying feet, the clinking of baskets, and the rustling of wrapping paper filled the air as the town braced itself for the day's festivities.

Down in the heart of the town, Mrs. Pendle's bakery hummed with activity, as a sweet, yeasty aroma of freshly baked bread and hot cross buns wafted from the open door. Mrs. Pendle herself, a stout woman with rosy cheeks and a loud laugh, was stacking trays of lemon tarts with the care of a mother cradling a child. She paused for a moment to peer out the window, her brows furrowing slightly as her gaze lingered on the far side of the square. She had heard the gossip. No one could ignore the strange figure who had appeared the day before, nor could they ignore the perfect eggs he had left behind.

'Odd, isn't it?' she muttered to herself, then quickly shook her head. 'I'm sure it's nothing.'

But a small, nagging doubt pulled at her, and she couldn't help but glance out the window again, as if the man might reappear at any moment.

Nearby, young Henry Pendle, Mrs. Pendle's youngest son, was practically bouncing with excitement as he darted around the square, practically dragging his older sister, Ellie, by the sleeve.

'Ellie! Ellie!' he called, grinning ear to ear. 'We're going to find all the eggs this year. Just you wait!'

Ellie, who was busy stuffing some leftover decorations into the back of a cart, only half-listened. She gave her brother a distracted smile and patted him on the head. 'I'm sure you will, Henry,' she said, but there was a slight frown on her face as she surveyed the square. 'You know, I heard the most curious thing this morning,' she added in a voice that was far too serious for such a playful occasion. 'Some people are saying the eggs aren't just eggs. They're... I don't know, enchanted or something.'

Henry laughed at the thought. 'Enchanted eggs? Come off it, Ellie! You're getting as bad as Dad, telling stories of ghosts and goblins.' He dashed off toward the group of children gathered by the post office, leaving Ellie to stare after him, a shiver running down her spine.

The square was beginning to fill with children, all chattering excitedly about the upcoming hunt. Some were skipping about in circles, their baskets already clutched in eager hands, while others nervously adjusted their Easter bonnets, eyeing the eggs that were hidden here and there, gleaming in the grass like jewels.

Among the bustling children, there were two in particular who stood out - Lily Rosewell and Max Thorndyke.

Lily, with her glossy curls and rosy cheeks, was a picture of perfection. She wore a pale pink dress, dotted with delicate lace, and a ribbon tied neatly beneath her chin. Her basket was woven from the finest straw, embroidered with little white flowers, and she was already eyeing the eggs in the distance as if she owned them. Max Thorndyke, her constant companion, was not far behind, his dark hair combed to within an inch of its life, his clothes pressed, and his expression one of quiet superiority.

Lily bent over, taking a quick glance to ensure no one was watching before she reached out to touch one of the eggs tucked beneath a nearby bush. 'I bet I'll find the prettiest ones,' she said to

Max, her voice dripping with confidence. 'No one else has the taste I do. These eggs will be all mine.'

Max, a spoiled child with a tendency toward smugness, straightened his collar and nodded. 'I'm sure you're right. You always find the best, Lily.' He glanced around to make sure no other children were nearby, his eyes narrowing in distaste when he noticed Sophie and Henry crossing the square.

'They're so *silly*, aren't they?' Max muttered, flicking a speck of dirt off his sleeve. 'Running around like headless chickens. They'll never find the best eggs. Not like us.'

Lily chuckled, but there was a touch of venom in her voice. 'They don't deserve them. Not when they're so... ordinary.'

The children watched as Sophie, a quiet, kind-hearted girl with a calm presence, moved across the square with Henry, who was practically jumping out of his shoes with excitement. Sophie was wearing a modest dress of pale blue, a ribbon tucked neatly in her hair. Her eyes sparkled, but there was no arrogance in her manner - only a simple joy in the act of playing and sharing with her friends.

'Look, Henry!' she said, pointing toward a patch of daffodils by the fountain. 'I see one hiding there!'

Henry, not one to be deterred by the beautiful but distant-looking eggs, was already charging toward the flowers, his laughter ringing through the square. Sophie followed more slowly, her eyes scanning the area. She wasn't interested in finding the most beautiful eggs - she was simply looking for any eggs that might be hidden where others couldn't see them, so she could share them with those who might not have the luck to find one.

But as they reached the spot by the fountain, Sophie's gaze drifted, and she spotted something curious - an egg that, rather than shimmering with intricate designs, was dull and almost weathered-looking. It was nestled just beneath the roots of a tree, barely noticeable amidst the tangled grass. Sophie knelt down, carefully brushing aside the foliage, and retrieved it. The egg was not the least bit grand - no painted swirls or sparkling glitter - but there was something warm and inviting about it, almost as though it had been placed there with great care.

Henry, who had already found a vibrant, beautifully decorated egg, was now turning to Sophie with a proud grin. 'Look at mine, Soph! Isn't it amazing? I bet I'll win the whole hunt with this one!' he boasted, holding it up for her to see.

Sophie smiled, but her eyes lingered on the plain egg in her hands. 'I think we should just enjoy the hunt, Henry,' she said gently. 'It's not always about winning, is it?'

Max and Lily, who had been observing from a distance, exchanged a quick look. There was something odd about Sophie's choice, but they were too wrapped up in their own hunt to dwell on it for long.

As the children scattered once more, the town square buzzed with the anticipation of the hunt. Yet, behind the excitement, the whispers about the stranger's eggs grew louder. Some of the parents exchanged nervous glances as they watched their children eagerly run about. Was it possible that those eggs were more than just a simple Easter treat? Was there something else at play here?

And in the middle of it all, the mysterious figure had not been seen again, though his presence lingered in the air, casting a shadow over the day's festivities. The adults, unsure whether to voice their suspicions aloud, went about their preparations with a sense of unease. But the children - blissfully unaware - were filled only with excitement and wonder, their baskets swinging wildly as they raced toward the next hidden treasure.

And so, the town of Maplewood continued its preparations for the Easter Egg Hunt, with both hope and doubt in the air, the line between joy and concern growing ever thinner with each passing moment.

CHAPTER THREE

The First Eggs

The sun was high in the sky by the time the Easter Egg Hunt officially began, casting long, golden beams across the town square. The excitement was palpable - every child in Maplewood had gathered, baskets clutched tightly in their hands, eager for the adventure ahead. Parents stood on the sidelines, watching with fond smiles, though a few cast wary glances toward the far corners of the square, where the stranger's eggs had first been found.

But none of the children seemed to notice, so caught up were they in the fun. The hunt had started, and there was no time to waste.

Sophie stood at the edge of the square, her heart fluttering with a quiet joy. She had never been one for the competition that usually accompanied the hunt, preferring to quietly enjoy the simple pleasure of it all. Her basket, made of woven straw and decorated with a delicate ribbon, swung gently at her side as she looked out across the grassy lawn, where the first of the eggs had been placed.

Henry, his red hair tousled and his freckles glowing in the sunshine, bounced beside her, practically vibrating with energy. He didn't share Sophie's calm approach to the hunt. 'Last one to the fountain is a rotten egg!' he shouted, before sprinting off without so much as a glance over his shoulder.

Sophie laughed and shook her head. She wasn't about to chase after Henry - he'd always been the one to rush headlong into everything, from races to pranks. But that was Henry - full of life, eager to dive headfirst into whatever adventure came his way.

The children scattered like confetti, their laughter filling the air as they dashed across the square and into the gardens, their eyes scanning for the treasure that lay hidden beneath bushes, behind trees, and under flowerpots. Some children moved in groups, chattering excitedly as they scoured the grounds, while others, like Sophie, wandered on their own, savouring the thrill of the search rather than the competition.

It wasn't long before Sophie spotted her first egg.

It was tucked in the corner of a garden bed, just beneath the twisting vine of a climbing rose. The egg was plain - unadorned, almost as if it had been forgotten by the stranger himself. Its pale, speckled surface was unremarkable, and it looked like something anyone might have overlooked in their haste to find the glimmering, more ornate eggs scattered throughout the square.

Sophie's brow furrowed slightly as she knelt down to pick it up. She had expected something more... well, magical. But there was a quiet charm to it, something that made her smile as she cradled it in her hands. Perhaps there was more to Easter eggs than glittering shells and perfect patterns.

Behind her, Henry shouted in triumph, his voice high and wild. 'Found one! Found one!'

Sophie turned just in time to see him proudly holding up a large egg, shimmering with gold and pink swirls that sparkled like the stars. The egg practically glowed in the sunlight, so vibrant and eye-catching that even Sophie couldn't help but pause for a moment to admire it.

'Isn't it amazing?' Henry grinned, practically bursting with pride. 'I bet this one's filled with chocolate!'

Sophie smiled at him, though there was a small twist of unease in her chest. She wasn't sure why, but she felt a strange sensation, as though the egg in Henry's hands were too perfect. There was something... unsettling about it, though she couldn't explain why.

Henry, oblivious to the flicker of doubt in his sister's eyes, bounded off toward the fountain, searching for more. Sophie turned back to her own egg, brushing the dirt from its surface with a gentle thumb. The more she held it, the more she felt it was just right.

THE EASTER EGG HUNT

Meanwhile, over near the far side of the square, Lily and Max were already making their way toward a patch of flowers, eyes narrowed with the determination of treasure hunters. Lily's dress, now a little wrinkled from her earlier excitement, swished around her legs as she marched toward a bush in the corner of the garden. Her golden curls bounced with each step, and Max was right behind her, scowling at anyone who dared get too close.

'Move it!' Max muttered to a pair of younger children who had wandered into his path, shoving them aside without a second thought. 'We're finding the best eggs today. Not the dull ones - those are for babies.'

Lily smirked at him, flicking a strand of hair from her face. 'You're right. I bet we'll find all the best ones. Look at this one, Max!' She held up a large, opulent egg, decorated in swirls of ruby red, silver stars, and delicate gold vines that seemed to shimmer with a life of their own.

Max grinned, his eyes gleaming with pride. 'That's the one. I knew it was going to be this egg.'

They both looked down at the egg with the same greedy gleam in their eyes, both children so absorbed in their find that they didn't even notice the small group of children watching them from a distance.

But Sophie did. She had wandered closer, curious about their finds, when she overheard Lily and Max boasting in loud whispers about the 'perfect' eggs they had discovered.

'Oh, it's definitely filled with something magical,' Lily declared, turning the egg over in her hands, her voice dripping with satisfaction. 'Look at the design! No one else will find one this beautiful, I just know it.'

Sophie, who had never been one to boast, felt a flicker of discomfort. She wasn't sure why, but something about their excitement - their certainty that only the most ornate, most beautiful eggs were worth anything - left her unsettled. She glanced down at the plain egg she still held in her basket, its smooth surface unmarked by decoration, its humble simplicity a stark contrast to the radiant eggs Lily and Max now held in their hands.

Meanwhile, Henry had found another egg - this one a gleaming blue, with intricate white patterns swirling around it. He ran over to Sophie, his face flushed with triumph.

'Look, Soph! Isn't it brilliant?' he cried, holding it up to her with sparkling eyes.

Sophie nodded, smiling at him, though she couldn't help but notice how the egg seemed almost too perfect, too deliberate in its design. She glanced back at the other children, noting the same gleaming, polished eggs that seemed to pop up in every corner of the square.

'Let's keep going,' she said softly, trying to shake the feeling gnawing at her. 'There's more to find. Maybe something else will be hidden where no one else looks.'

But even as Sophie moved on, a small voice inside her couldn't help but wonder: Was it the egg's exterior that mattered? Or was there something more to be found beneath the surface - something hidden beneath all the glitter and shine?

As the hunt continued, the first cracks in the day's cheerful veneer began to show. Some children, like Lily and Max, were consumed with finding the most magnificent eggs, their boastful laughter ringing through the square. Others, like Sophie and Henry, remained focused on the joy of discovery itself, regardless of how their finds appeared. The contrast between the children's choices - and their actions - had already begun to tell a story that no one, not even the children themselves, could yet fully understand.

CHAPTER FOUR

The Rotten Inside

The air was thick with the sound of laughter and shouting as the Easter Egg Hunt reached its peak. Children raced from one end of the square to the other, their baskets brimming with colourful eggs, the contents of which remained a tantalising mystery for now. The sun hung low in the sky, casting a warm glow over the scene, but even the bright light could not chase away the growing tension among the children.

Lily and Max, having claimed a treasure trove of the most exquisitely decorated eggs, were standing together in the shade of a large oak tree, admiring their prizes. They were so caught up in the dazzling beauty of the eggs that they hardly noticed the murmur of children around them, discussing their finds with a mixture of awe and uncertainty. For Lily and Max, nothing else mattered - only the thrill of having the most magnificent eggs of all.

Lily raised her egg, the one with the ruby-red swirls and gold vines, to her lips, a self-satisfied smirk tugging at her mouth. 'I told you, Max. This one's going to be perfect. Just wait and see.'

Max was already eyeing his own egg, a blue-and-silver creation that shimmered in the afternoon light. He gave it a quick lick of his lips, his excitement barely contained. 'We're going to be the envy of everyone, Lily. I bet it's filled with chocolate. Or maybe caramel. Something sweet, something special.'

With a synchronised nod, both children bit into their eggs at the same time, eager to taste the delights within.

At first, all was quiet, save for the gentle crunching sound as they bit into the eggshells. But the moment the insides touched their tongues, both Lily and Max recoiled in horror.

Lily's face contorted in disgust. She gagged, her hand flying to her mouth as she spat out the vile taste that had invaded her senses. 'Ugh! What is that?!' she shrieked, her voice rising in panic. Her eyes watered as the rotten, foul taste of decay lingered on her tongue, filling her with nausea.

Max wasn't far behind. He had barely swallowed a mouthful before his stomach lurched, and he, too, was spitting the contents out, his face pale with shock. 'This... this is awful!' he gasped, clutching his stomach as if trying to will away the sickening feeling that was rapidly spreading through his body. He blinked furiously, his eyes watering with the strength of his revulsion.

The two children stumbled back from each other, their faces twisted with horror as they tossed the eggs aside, their hands shaking. They looked at each other, eyes wide with disbelief, before Lily let out a shrill cry.

'Why is it like this?' she wailed, her voice trembling. 'It was so perfect on the outside! What's wrong with it?!'

Max, still holding his stomach, could barely answer, the sour taste still clinging to his mouth. 'I... I don't know,' he muttered, his usual arrogance replaced by confusion and a growing sense of panic.

Meanwhile, Sophie and Henry, who had wandered a little farther down the square, were happily munching on their own finds. Sophie had chosen the plain, speckled egg that she had discovered beneath the rose bush earlier, and Henry had picked a blue egg - less flashy than some of the others, but just as intriguing. They sat on a bench, their baskets at their feet, sharing their discoveries with each other.

As Sophie bit into her egg, she was met with an explosion of sweetness that made her eyes widen in surprise. It was delicious, far more so than she had expected. The filling was smooth and creamy, with hints of caramel and vanilla that danced on her tongue. She closed her eyes, savouring the taste.

'This is incredible,' she whispered to herself, a smile tugging at the corners of her lips.

THE EASTER EGG HUNT

Henry, already several bites into his own egg, was grinning ear to ear. 'You were right, Soph,' he said through a mouthful of sweet, gooey goodness. 'This egg's got the best filling ever! It's better than chocolate, even!'

Sophie, always thoughtful, nodded but said nothing. There was something more to this than just a tasty treat. She felt a strange sense of satisfaction, but not from the deliciousness alone. She looked down at the plain egg she had chosen, feeling a quiet comfort in its simplicity. There was nothing flashy about it, but it had turned out to be perfect in its own way.

As they sat there, other children began to trickle over, drawn by the scent of the sweets that seemed to be emanating from Sophie and Henry's eggs. A group of them, led by young Ellie Pendle, who had found a modest egg of her own, gathered around them, their curiosity piqued.

'What are you eating?' Ellie asked, her eyes wide with interest. 'It smells amazing!'

Sophie smiled and held out the egg for her to see. 'It's the one I found under the rose bush,' she said. 'It's not decorated like the others, but the inside... well, it's the best thing I've ever tasted.'

Ellie bit into her own egg, her face lighting up with joy as the sweet flavour unfolded on her tongue. 'You're right!' she exclaimed. 'It's like... like a sugar cloud! So soft, and... and warm, almost!'

Soon, other children, who had been struggling with their own finds, began to wander over. Henry, grinning, broke off a piece of his own egg and offered it to a younger boy who had been sitting quietly to the side, looking disappointed at the more ordinary eggs he had collected. The boy took a tentative bite, and then his face lit up in surprise. 'This... this is *amazing*! Where did you get it?'

Sophie smiled gently. 'We found ours in the corner of the square. Maybe... maybe the plain eggs are the ones that have the best surprises inside.'

But just as the children were beginning to share their sweet discoveries, the noise of distress grew louder. Lily, her face red with fury, was shouting at Max. 'Why didn't we get one like theirs, Max? Why?' she wailed. 'This is unfair!'

Max was equally distraught, glaring at the rotten egg lying forgotten on the ground beside him. 'It's... it's not supposed to be like this,' he muttered. 'I don't understand. It looked perfect. What's wrong with it?'

Around them, the other children exchanged bewildered glances. Some were still munching on their sweet eggs, their expressions a mix of joy and confusion, while others, like Lily and Max, stood in silent shock, staring at the wreckage of their once-prized eggs.

'Maybe it's because we wanted the best ones,' said Sophie softly, her voice tinged with sympathy. She glanced over at Lily and Max, feeling a twinge of pity for them despite their earlier boasting. 'Sometimes, what looks the best isn't always the best. You have to look deeper, I think.'

At that moment, the children's eyes fell on a figure standing at the edge of the square. The stranger, in his long coat and wide-brimmed hat, was watching them from a distance. His face was obscured in shadow, but his eyes gleamed with quiet satisfaction, as if he knew exactly what had unfolded.

Sophie felt a shiver run down her spine as she met his gaze for the briefest of moments. There was no anger or malice in his expression, only the calm, knowing smile of someone who had set a test and watched it unfold.

And then, just as quickly as he had appeared, the stranger turned and melted back into the crowd, his figure disappearing like a dream.

For a moment, everything was still. And then, as if waking from a trance, the children turned back to their eggs, their minds racing as they began to understand the lesson that had been laid before them - hidden within the simple and the beautiful, within the rotten and the sweet.

THE EASTER EGG HUNT

And in the distance, the stranger watched them, his eyes gleaming brighter than ever before.

CHAPTER FIVE

The Lesson Begins

The air in the town square had turned heavy with confusion. What had started as a joyful Easter Egg Hunt, filled with laughter and excitement, had quickly soured into a hushed murmur of bewilderment and frustration. The children stood scattered about, staring down at their baskets, their faces furrowed in puzzlement and anger, as they tried to make sense of what had just happened.

Sophie and Henry sat on the edge of the fountain, their baskets still full of the plain eggs they had found, while the other children began to disperse. Sophie glanced over at the group of children who had been so thrilled with their decorated eggs earlier - Lily, Max, and the others. They were now huddled together, their eyes cast downward, their faces red with fury or humiliation.

'Why did it taste like that?' Lily's voice rang out sharply, cutting through the silence. She was standing with her arms crossed, her cheeks flushed with indignation. 'It wasn't supposed to be like that! It was supposed to be perfect!'

Max stood beside her, his jaw clenched in frustration, glaring down at the remains of the rotten egg on the ground as if willing it to change. 'It's not fair,' he muttered darkly, kicking a stone with force. 'I deserved better than this. We always get the best, don't we?'

Sophie, watching them from her perch by the fountain, exchanged a quiet look with Henry. He gave a small shrug, the corners of his mouth still curled in a hint of a smile, though it wasn't one of triumph. 'I think we need to talk to them,' he said softly.

Sophie nodded, her expression thoughtful. She didn't feel smug or satisfied - she felt... concerned. She had seen the looks on their faces, the way they clutched their baskets as if trying to protect themselves from the discomfort of the situation. The lesson, though clear to her, hadn't quite sunk in for everyone else.

With a deep breath, Sophie stood up, smoothing down the folds of her simple dress. 'Come on, Henry. Let's go.'

The two children walked toward Lily, Max, and the others, who were gathered in a tight-knit group, muttering in frustration.

'I can't believe this,' Lily was saying, her voice sharp with anger. 'I never pick the wrong thing! Never. This is ridiculous. It's just bad luck, that's all. Someone must've switched the eggs on us.'

Max nodded fiercely, though his eyes darted about nervously as though searching for someone to blame. 'Exactly! It's like they were cursed or something. There's no way they were meant to be like that. We didn't do anything wrong.'

Sophie approached cautiously, her voice soft yet steady. 'Lily... Max... it wasn't bad luck.'

Lily spun around, her face flushed with frustration and disbelief. 'What do you mean? How can it not be bad luck? I got the perfect egg, and it turned out disgusting! That's not fair!'

Sophie took a deep breath, her voice calm and patient. 'I know it's hard to understand, but sometimes things aren't as they seem on the outside. You know, the eggs you picked... they were beautiful on the outside, right? But the inside... well, they weren't what you thought they were.'

Max's brow furrowed, his lips curled in a scowl. 'And what about yours, then? Yours weren't decorated, but they tasted great. How does that make sense?'

Sophie hesitated, then glanced over at Henry, who was standing a little further off, watching the conversation unfold. He gave her a small nod, and she felt a surge of courage. She turned back to Lily and Max, her voice gentle but firm.

'It's not about how things look. It's about what's inside,' Sophie said. 'The eggs you picked were shiny and pretty, but inside... they weren't good. Maybe because the outside mattered too much to you. But Henry and I chose eggs that looked simple - plain even - but they turned out to be sweet, just like they were meant to be. Sometimes the best things come from what's not immediately obvious. You have to look deeper.'

Max opened his mouth to argue, but Sophie raised her hand to stop him, her tone soft but insistent.

'I know it's hard to accept,' she continued. 'But... the lesson here is that what's on the outside doesn't tell the whole story. You can't judge something - *or someone* - just by how they appear. The eggs were only part of it. The real lesson... is about how we treat others, and how we see the world. What matters most is what's inside.'

Lily's face was still flushed with anger, but now there was a flicker of uncertainty in her eyes. She opened her mouth to speak, but the words seemed to catch in her throat. Instead, she pressed her lips together and glared at the ground, clearly trying to hold back the frustration bubbling within her.

Max, though, wasn't so quick to soften. He scowled at Sophie, his voice dripping with sarcasm. 'So, you're saying we deserve the rotten eggs because we're... what? Not good enough?' He gave a bitter laugh. 'Well, I think I'd rather just have bad luck than listen to a silly story about "inner beauty."'

Sophie's heart clenched at the bitterness in his voice, but she refused to let his words shake her. 'It's not about deserving anything,' she said quietly. 'It's about learning. You don't have to be perfect on the outside, or have the most expensive or fancy things, to be a good person. What matters is how you treat others, how you choose to be kind, and how you see the world. True beauty - true goodness - comes from within.'

For a long moment, there was nothing but silence between the children. The only sounds were the rustling of leaves in the wind and the distant laughter of other children who were still finishing their hunts, their baskets full of eggs both plain and beautiful.

Sophie watched Lily and Max carefully, wondering if her words were sinking in, even a little.

Max finally broke the silence, his voice gruff. 'I don't care about that,' he muttered, though there was an edge of uncertainty creeping into his tone. 'I just wanted the best.'

Sophie nodded, offering a small, understanding smile. 'I know. But sometimes the 'best' isn't what you think it is. And sometimes, what we want isn't always what we need.'

Lily, still standing with her arms crossed, looked up at Sophie, her gaze more thoughtful than before. 'So... you're saying... I should have chosen one of those plain eggs like yours?' she asked, her voice quieter now, less sharp.

Sophie nodded. 'I think... maybe it's about choosing things for the right reasons. And being willing to accept that sometimes what looks the best on the outside doesn't always feel the best on the inside.'

Lily stood there, her arms uncrossing as she chewed on Sophie's words. There was no easy answer, no immediate fix. But Sophie could see the seed of understanding beginning to take root.

Max, still muttering under his breath, turned to walk away, but not before shooting one last, half-hearted glare at Sophie and Henry. 'You're lucky you got good eggs,' he grumbled, his voice thick with pride and bitterness. 'But I'm not going to forget this.'

Sophie's smile faded slightly, but she didn't let the harshness of his words disturb her. It would take time, she knew. Some lessons were harder to learn than others.

As Max stormed off with Lily in tow, Sophie sat back down on the fountain, her basket of eggs resting in her lap. She glanced up at Henry, who had been quietly observing the exchange, his expression thoughtful.

'Do you think they'll understand?' Sophie asked softly.

Henry shrugged, offering a small, but hopeful smile. 'Maybe. It's a start, at least.'

Sophie nodded, staring into the distance. There was still much to learn. But for now, in the quiet of the town square, amidst the Easter sunshine, the lesson had begun.

CHAPTER SIX

The Second Round

The sun hung high in the sky, the warmth of the early afternoon casting a golden glow over Maplewood. The town square had once again come alive with the sound of excited voices and the clatter of footsteps on cobblestones. The Easter Egg Hunt had resumed, and the children, still abuzz with the memory of the first round, scattered across the square to find new treasures. But this time, something was different. This time, the children were wiser.

Sophie adjusted the strap of her basket, her gaze sweeping the familiar corners of the town square, where she had discovered so many surprises the day before. She could already hear the chatter of children echoing through the air as they set off in search of eggs, but there was a new undercurrent to their voices - a sense of anticipation, tempered by caution. They had learned the hard way that things weren't always as they seemed, and the children who had been so eager for the most dazzling eggs before now took a more careful approach.

'Do you think they'll taste good again?' Henry asked, his eyes twinkling with curiosity as he hefted his small basket, which was already half full of the simple eggs he'd picked.

Sophie smiled at him, the warmth of their earlier conversation still lingering. 'I think so. We've learned our lesson. We know what to look for now.'

They walked toward the far corner of the square, Sophie's hand lightly brushing the leaves of the trees that shaded the path. The scent of fresh grass and blooming flowers mixed with the soft breeze that carried the echoes of the hunt in the air. It felt almost magical - like the world itself was holding its breath, waiting for the next surprise to unfold.

Henry, ever eager, darted ahead, his red hair bouncing with each stride. 'Come on, Sophie! Let's see if we can find the really good ones this time.'

Sophie followed at a slower pace, her steps light and thoughtful. She had already made up her mind. She would stick to the plain eggs. No matter how beautiful the others were, no matter how much they tempted her, she knew that beauty was only skin deep. After all, the best surprises were often hidden beneath the surface, and those were the eggs she would trust.

As they reached the next patch of grass near the fountain, Sophie spotted a plain, dull-looking egg nestled under a stone bench. It was speckled, its colour muted and unremarkable - exactly the sort of egg most children would ignore in favour of the more ornate ones. Sophie smiled and crouched down to retrieve it, her fingers brushing the cool surface of the egg.

'I've got one,' she called to Henry, holding it up with a sense of quiet pride. It was, in its own way, perfect.

Henry, already off in search of his next find, waved without looking back. 'Great! I'm going for the gold ones today. Let's see if they're as good as they look!'

Sophie shook her head, but there was no judgment in her smile. Henry was still learning, just as the others were. He had his own path to follow, just as everyone did.

At the far end of the square, Lily and Max were already at it again. The two children were deep in conversation, their eyes scanning the lawn with practiced precision. They were still searching for the most glamorous, eye-catching eggs - eggs that sparkled in the sunlight, eggs that screamed perfect in the way they glittered and glowed.

'There's one!' Max pointed excitedly at an egg nestled among the thick roots of a tree. The egg was a deep, rich purple, streaked with silver that shimmered like moonlight. It was the kind of egg that would make anyone's heart race with excitement - if they didn't already know the lessons of the hunt.

'Don't touch it, Max!' Lily snapped, a little too loudly for Sophie's liking. 'I saw it first!'

Max's face flushed with irritation, but he shrugged it off. 'I don't care. It's mine now.'

Sophie watched them as they bickered, her chest tightening with sympathy. It was clear that they hadn't yet learned the lesson that had begun to sink into the hearts of the other children. For them, the outer beauty of the eggs still mattered more than what was inside. They still believed that the most magnificent eggs would bring the best rewards, no matter what had happened the day before.

'I'm sure it'll taste lovely,' Lily was muttering to herself, her fingers already brushing the smooth surface of the purple egg as if she could already feel the sweetness inside. 'It looks like it's filled with the best filling. There's no way it's rotten.'

Max grinned, his eyes gleaming with the confidence that only an ego bruised by defeat could summon. 'It's definitely the best one. I'm not making the same mistake again.'

Sophie turned away, shaking her head but feeling a little sad for them. They hadn't yet grasped the truth: that *inside* mattered far more than *outside*. They hadn't yet seen the pattern - the truth that the eggs that seemed perfect on the surface were, more often than not, the ones that disappointed.

With a sigh, Sophie moved further down the path. It wasn't for her to fix, not today. She had to let them discover the lesson on their own, as hard as it might be.

***

As the hunt wore on, the contrast between the reactions of the children grew even starker. Sophie, Henry, and their friends continued to find the plain, unadorned eggs - eggs that seemed so unassuming at first glance, but revealed their delicious secrets when cracked open. Sophie had found a pale-yellow egg near the edge of the square, and when she cracked it open, she was met with a filling so sweet and creamy that she could hardly believe it. Henry, too, had discovered another unembellished egg that turned out to be filled with a rich, honeyed sweetness. Both children shared their discoveries with those around them, who, seeing their joy, hesitated no longer and chose their own simple eggs.

Ellie, the youngest of the group, found a dull grey egg under a cluster of bushes and, to her surprise, found it filled with the most delicate chocolate ganache. Her face lit up with wonder as she shared it with the others.

'See?' Sophie smiled at her. 'Sometimes, the best surprises are hidden away in the simplest things.'

But over on the other side of the square, the children who had clung to their desire for the most beautiful eggs were starting to show signs of discontent. Lily and Max were now furiously spitting out the foul-tasting fillings from their glittering eggs, their faces contorted in frustration.

'This is ridiculous!' Lily cried, her voice trembling with the force of her indignation. 'Why does it always happen to us?'

Max kicked the ground angrily, his basket half full of brightly decorated eggs that had proven to be nothing but disappointment. 'I knew it,' he muttered, though his words lacked conviction. 'It's not fair. We should've gotten something better.'

Lily's hands trembled as she held up a third egg, its surface gleaming with brilliant gold. 'This one's perfect. I just know it will taste good.'

But when she bit into it, the look of disgust that crossed her face was undeniable. The egg was rancid - its insides spoiled, no sweetness to be found.

Sophie, watching from a distance, felt a pang of empathy for them, even if they didn't yet understand. It was a hard lesson to learn, the hardest kind of lesson: that what you desire isn't always what you need.

With a sigh, she turned back to Henry and the others, who were happily exchanging their simple eggs and tasting the sweet rewards inside. Their joy was contagious, filling the air with an energy that only true understanding could bring.

The second round of the hunt had shown everyone what they needed to see. The pretty eggs, once again, were filled with disappointment. The plain eggs, however - those unadorned treasures - held the sweetest surprises.

And though Lily and Max were still stumbling through their frustration, the others were beginning to realise the truth, sometimes, it's the simplest things that offer the greatest rewards.

Sophie smiled to herself, feeling a quiet sense of satisfaction. There was still much to learn, but the lesson had begun to take root.

CHAPTER SEVEN

The Stranger's Revelation

The sun had begun to dip below the horizon, casting a warm, amber light over the town of Maplewood. The Easter Egg Hunt, which had started with such excitement and anticipation, had come to an end. Children gathered in small clusters, comparing their findings, their voices rising and falling with a mixture of wonder and disappointment. Most were still sorting through their baskets, some triumphantly holding up their plain eggs as if they had just discovered hidden treasures. Others, like Lily and Max, were sulking off to the side, their glittering eggs abandoned in disgust, their faces clouded with the bitter taste of failure.

Sophie, Henry, and their friends stood together near the fountain, their baskets now filled with the simplest, most unadorned eggs. Their faces were bright with smiles, a quiet sense of satisfaction lingering in the air around them. They had learned their lesson. They understood that what was on the outside didn't matter as much as what lay within.

And yet, there was something more - something about the entire hunt that still felt unfinished. It was as if there was a part of the mystery still waiting to be revealed.

Then, like a shadow falling across the square, the stranger appeared. The man in the long, dark coat and wide-brimmed hat stood at the far end of the square, his figure an enigmatic silhouette against the soft evening light. As always, there was something both unsettling and compelling about him. His presence, though quiet, seemed to draw the attention of every child in the square.

'Gather round,' the stranger's voice, low and steady, rang out across the square.

THE EASTER EGG HUNT

Without a word, the children, as though moved by some unseen force, began to gather around him. Sophie, Henry, and the others looked at each other in confusion. They had all but forgotten about the stranger, so absorbed had they become in their discoveries. But now, with the sun setting behind him, he seemed like a figure who had been waiting for this moment all along.

Lily and Max, though still muttering to each other, reluctantly joined the group, their faces still red from the bitter taste of the rotten eggs. Even they couldn't ignore the pull of the stranger's presence.

'Why are we all gathered here?' Max asked, his tone sharp but curious. 'What does this have to do with the eggs?'

The stranger's gaze fell upon him, his dark eyes glimmering in the fading light. 'Everything, young one,' he replied, his voice soft but carrying a weight that made the air feel stiller, as though the earth itself was listening. 'It has everything to do with the eggs.'

The children fell silent, watching him closely, waiting for an explanation that, somehow, they had all known was coming.

He stepped forward, his long coat trailing behind him like a shadow. His voice became quieter, but no less compelling, as he spoke.

'The eggs you have found today,' he began, 'were never meant to be magical in the way you might think. They were not enchanted with spells or powers, but rather, they reflected something much more important, the hearts of those who chose them.'

A murmur rippled through the crowd of children, a mix of confusion and intrigue. Sophie frowned, her brow furrowing as she exchanged a glance with Henry. Was that what the eggs had been? A reflection of... their hearts?

'Each of you,' the stranger continued, 'picked the eggs that seemed to call to you. Some of you chose eggs that glittered and gleamed, that seemed perfect and precious. Others chose eggs that were plain, unadorned, and simple. But the true nature of the eggs has always been tied to one thing: your hearts.'

Lily's brow wrinkled, and she crossed her arms in defiance. 'What do you mean? I picked the eggs I wanted. The best ones. There's no magic in that.'

The stranger's lips curled into a faint smile, as though he were accustomed to such defiance. 'Ah, but that is where you're mistaken, my dear. The beautiful eggs - those that were dazzling in their appearance - were meant for those who, in their hearts, have been selfish, vain, or cruel. Those who seek to impress others, to make themselves seem more than they are, are often drawn to such things. They crave the outward beauty, not realising that the inside is spoiled, just as their hearts can sometimes be spoiled by their desires.'

Sophie felt a chill run down her spine, her hand instinctively reaching for the plain egg in her basket. It wasn't just the eggs - it was something deeper, something about the way they had been so eager to appear perfect, while their true nature had been hidden beneath.

Lily's face flushed with anger and confusion. 'But that's not fair! I deserved the best eggs! I always choose the best - everyone knows that!'

The stranger's eyes softened, as though he understood the pain in her voice. 'Perhaps you did, my dear. But true worth is not found in beauty alone, but in kindness, generosity, and goodness. The plain eggs you rejected, the ones you thought were unworthy, were meant for those with hearts full of goodness - those who give without expecting in return, who care for others, who see the world not through the lens of *what can I get*, but *how can I help*. Those eggs, though plain, were filled with the sweetest surprises, for those who understand that true beauty lies within.'

Sophie's heart swelled with understanding. She had known it all along - had known, even as she had picked those plain eggs, that they held something far more precious than what appeared on the surface. The sweetness, the kindness, had been inside the eggs - and it was that same sweetness that filled her heart as she looked around at the children standing beside her. Sophie had chosen kindness. And the eggs had reflected that choice.

The stranger turned his gaze toward Max, who had been silent for a moment, his eyes wide with uncertainty. 'And you, young Max,' he said softly, 'who so desperately sought the most beautiful eggs, believing them to be the best... What did you find inside?'

Max swallowed hard, his face contorting with frustration as he thought back to the rotten fillings that had filled his eggs. He had wanted to be admired, to have the best, but in the end, he had learned a painful truth.

'I didn't get anything good,' he admitted, his voice small and tinged with embarrassment. 'I thought... I thought I could just take the best and it would be enough. But it wasn't.'

The stranger nodded, his expression gentle. 'And now you understand. The beauty of an egg, or a person, is not in its surface. The true value is what lies inside, and that can only be seen through actions, through the way we treat others.'

Max lowered his head, the weight of the revelation settling upon him like a heavy cloak. He had wanted to be the best, to be seen as perfect, but now, he understood - true worth had never been in the dazzling appearance, but in the goodness of the heart.

The stranger paused, letting the silence linger for a moment before he spoke once more.

'Remember, children,' he said, his voice carrying the weight of ancient wisdom, 'appearances can deceive, and the world may try to convince you that beauty is only skin deep. But the truest magic - the magic that matters - is not in how something looks, but in how it makes you feel. In how it touches your heart. And that, children, is the magic you carry within yourselves.'

With those final words, the stranger tipped his wide-brimmed hat and turned, disappearing into the gathering twilight, his figure blending with the shadows of the square. The children stood in silence, processing his words, feeling the quiet weight of the lesson that had been shared with them.

Sophie, her heart full, looked at Henry, who smiled back at her. The day's hunt, the stranger's words - they had all pointed to one simple truth.

True beauty, true worth, had always been inside them all along.

CHAPTER EIGHT

A Town Transformed

The evening sky deepened into hues of lavender and twilight blue as the last of the children trickled out of the town square. The Easter Egg Hunt was officially over, but the quiet murmur of reflection seemed to linger in the air, as if the town itself had taken a collective breath and was about to exhale into something new.

Sophie and Henry, hands still clutching their baskets, walked side by side down the cobbled streets, their faces flushed with a sense of quiet triumph - not from the eggs they had collected, but from the understanding they had gained. The world felt a little different now. Softer, somehow. As if the sharp edges of the day had been smoothed out by the lesson they had learned.

'I never thought about it that way before,' Henry said thoughtfully, breaking the silence that had settled between them.

Sophie smiled up at him, her eyes reflecting the last rays of sunlight. 'Neither did I. But it makes sense, doesn't it? What matters is how we treat others... not how we look or what we have.'

'Yeah,' Henry agreed, looking down at the plain egg he'd carefully placed in his basket. He turned it over in his hand, as though noticing it for the first time. 'I think I'll keep this one. It's my favourite.'

As they reached the edge of the square, they saw a group of children gathered by the fountain, including Lily and Max. The two children, who had been so confident in their glittering eggs earlier, now looked smaller somehow, as though the weight of the day's lessons had made them reconsider everything they had once thought was important.

Lily was the first to break the silence between them. Her usual haughty demeanour was gone, replaced by an air of humility that Sophie had never seen before. She glanced at Sophie, Henry, and the others with a mix of uncertainty and resolve.

'I...' Lily began, her voice wavering slightly. 'I... I'm sorry. I know I was awful today. And before today, too. I thought that because I had the most beautiful eggs, I'd be the most important. But... I see now that I was wrong. I hurt people. I made them feel bad about themselves, just so I could feel good.'

Max, standing next to her, shifted uncomfortably but nodded. 'I didn't think about anyone else. All I cared about was having the best. I thought that if I had the perfect eggs, everyone would like me more. But... well, that didn't work out, did it?'

Sophie and Henry exchanged a glance. There was no trace of malice in Lily and Max's voices now. No boasting or arrogance. Just a quiet sincerity.

'It's okay,' Sophie said softly. 'I know you didn't mean to hurt anyone. We just... we didn't understand, did we? But now we do.'

Lily's eyes brightened, and she smiled - just a little. 'I guess we've learned something today, haven't we?'

Max's smile, though small, was genuine. 'Yeah... and maybe next year, I'll try looking for plain eggs.'

Sophie laughed lightly. 'I think you'll find they're the best kind.'

And just like that, something shifted. What had once been a town divided - those who craved outward perfection and those who saw the beauty in simplicity - now found a quiet unity. The air seemed lighter, as if the very fabric of Maplewood had been infused with something new. A spirit of kindness, of understanding, of shared experience.

As the children dispersed, Sophie and Henry made their way to the heart of the square, where the townsfolk were slowly beginning to emerge from their homes, drawn by the gathering of children and the soft glow of lanterns.

THE EASTER EGG HUNT

It was then that Sophie noticed something remarkable. The adults - who had once looked on with indifference, or worse, with judgment - now spoke to one another with a quiet warmth. Mrs. Wilkins, the bakery owner, who had always been too busy to chat, was smiling as she handed out slices of her famous lemon cake to the children, encouraging them to take more. Mr. Jenkins, the shopkeeper, who'd once grumbled about the egg hunt being a waste of time, was chuckling with his neighbours, his arms full of baskets of freshly picked flowers that he had begun to distribute with surprising generosity.

And then there was Mayor Thompson, who had been the most reluctant to embrace the hunt in the first place. He stood in front of the gathering crowd, his face softer than it had been before, his voice carrying the same thoughtful tone that the children had heard earlier in the day.

'I've heard the news,' he said, his eyes scanning the crowd with a quiet, almost wistful look. 'About the eggs, about the lesson we've all learned today. I've always thought that perfection was what we should aim for in life - always striving to be better, to be more - but I see now that perhaps that isn't the point at all. Perhaps it's more important to be kind. To look inside, rather than out.'

The townsfolk nodded in agreement, and some exchanged glances, as though the town itself had just learned something too.

Sophie stood there, surrounded by friends, by children she barely knew, by adults who had long kept their distance. But in that moment, it didn't matter. The town was different. The spirit of Maplewood was different.

'Do you think,' Henry said quietly, 'that things will stay like this? I mean, will people really change?'

Sophie smiled, watching the adults converse with newfound warmth, the laughter of the children ringing out like music. 'I think... I think we'll all try our best,' she said. 'It's not always easy, but I think we're on the right track. If we remember that kindness matters more than what people look like, then we can change.'

Henry grinned. 'I think you're right.'

As the night drew on, the square buzzed with conversation, with laughter, with a sense of possibility that hadn't been there before. Sophie and Henry found themselves walking home, their baskets empty but their hearts full.

'You know,' Henry said as they approached Sophie's house, 'maybe next year, we'll leave some of the best eggs for the other kids.'

Sophie smiled, her heart light. 'I think that would be a good idea.'

And in the quiet of Maplewood, under the soft twinkling of the stars, it was clear, the town had been transformed. Not by magic, not by any spell or enchantment - but by the understanding that kindness was the truest form of beauty. That love, generosity, and honesty were the things that mattered most.

And as the children and the adults settled into their homes, a feeling of contentment hung in the air, as though the very heart of Maplewood had begun to beat in a new, gentler rhythm. A rhythm that would guide them all, year after year, towards a future built not on appearances, but on the goodness of the heart.

CHAPTER NINE

The Stranger's Departure

The morning after the Easter Egg Hunt, Maplewood awoke to a town that seemed just a little brighter, as if the very air carried a new energy. The children were laughing and playing in the streets with a newfound sense of camaraderie, their laughter light and free. Sophie and Henry met by the old oak tree near the square, as they had so many times before, but today something felt different, something deeper, as if the lessons of the past day had woven a quiet magic into the fabric of the town itself.

The streets, now covered in soft petals from the cherry blossoms, seemed to hum with a kind of peacefulness that hadn't been there before. It was as though the world had softened, the edges of the day made round and gentle, full of possibility. And yet, there was a question that lingered in the air, like a song unsung - one that neither Sophie nor Henry had dared to ask aloud, but that both felt keenly.

Where was the stranger?

He had come so suddenly, like a fleeting shadow on the edge of a dream, and now he was gone, as mysteriously as he had appeared. It was as if the very earth had swallowed him up, leaving behind no trace but the ripple of his presence. No one had seen him since the evening of the hunt, and yet his influence hung over Maplewood like the scent of fresh rain - subtle but unmistakable.

As Sophie and Henry stood there, their fingers intertwined in a silent, shared thought, a figure in the distance caught their eye. It was a tall man, dressed in a long, dark coat and wide-brimmed hat, walking at a deliberate pace toward the edge of town.

It was him. The stranger.

But he did not pause. He did not stop to speak to anyone. His stride was steady, purposeful, as though he had left his mark on the town and was now moving on to the next. The children stared at him, unable to move, watching as the man's silhouette grew smaller and smaller, until it was swallowed by the trees on the outskirts of Maplewood.

'He's really leaving,' Henry whispered, his voice tinged with awe. 'Just like that. No goodbye.'

Sophie nodded, feeling the strange sensation of loss tug at her chest, even though she knew it was the right thing. The stranger had come to teach them, and now, just as quietly, he was leaving. It felt as though the lesson he had imparted was still sinking in, working its way into the heart of the town, and in a way, that was all the goodbye they would need.

In the days that followed, life in Maplewood continued as it always had, but the change was undeniable. The town had shifted - no, transformed - into something more. The children, once quick to boast or compare, now played together with open hearts, sharing their toys and treats, offering a hand to help one another up when someone fell. They had learned the value of kindness, the beauty of generosity, and the importance of looking beyond the surface.

Lily, once known for her vanity, was seen holding hands with Max, guiding him as they picked wildflowers for the town's community garden. Her laughter rang out in the air, no longer tainted by the need for attention, but full of a genuine joy she had never known. Max, too, seemed lighter, his usual bravado replaced by a quiet sense of belonging.

Sophie and Henry, though they had always been good friends, noticed a shift in themselves as well. They were more patient with others, more understanding. They helped the younger children with their games, teaching them how to share, how to be kind, how to find the beauty in the simple things.

Even the adults seemed to have absorbed the lesson the stranger had left behind. Mrs. Wilkins, who had spent years running her bakery with a quiet intensity, now smiled more freely as she handed out warm loaves of bread to anyone who stopped by. Mr. Jenkins, the shopkeeper, greeted every customer with a genuine warmth, and more than once, Sophie overheard him giving advice to the younger generation on the importance of hard work and kindness.

And as for Mayor Thompson, the once-stern leader of the town, he had become a man of reflection. His speeches were filled with a new sense of humility, and he often took time to visit the children in the park, asking them about their day and listening to their ideas for how to make the town even better. It was clear to everyone that the stranger's lesson had taken root in his heart as well.

Weeks passed, and the whispers of the Easter Egg Hunt became part of the town's history, passed down through generations of children. Every spring, when the air began to warm and the first blossoms of the season appeared, the children of Maplewood would gather for the annual hunt, eager not only to search for eggs, but to remember the lessons they had learned - that kindness, generosity, and humility were the true treasures of life.

Though no one ever spoke of the stranger directly, his impact could still be felt in every corner of the town. The way the children treated one another. The way the adults had become more open, more empathetic. Maplewood, once a town known for its quiet beauty and picturesque streets, had become something more - something rare. It was a town where people looked at each other, not through the lens of what they could see, but through the heart of what they could feel. It was a town where the inside truly matched the outside.

Sophie, standing near the fountain one afternoon with Henry by her side, smiled as she watched a group of children share their Easter eggs with the little ones in the town square. The sun was setting, casting long shadows across the cobblestones, but there was warmth in the air, a quiet kind of magic that filled the space between every laugh, every shared word, every gesture of kindness.

'I think,' Sophie said softly, her voice just above a whisper, 'he knew this would happen. He knew we'd understand.'

Henry nodded, looking out across the square with a thoughtful expression. 'He didn't need to say goodbye. The lesson is enough.'

Sophie smiled, feeling her heart swell with gratitude. They would never forget the stranger - not the man in the long, dark coat and wide-brimmed hat, who had come to their town and changed it in a way that no one would ever be able to describe. The stranger had left no mark on the earth, no footprint in the dirt. But his legacy had planted itself in the hearts of everyone in Maplewood.

And that, Sophie thought, was the most lasting magic of all.

As the sun set behind the town, casting its golden glow over the rooftops, Maplewood seemed to glow with a quiet warmth that could only be explained by the kindness and understanding that had bloomed in the hearts of all who lived there. The stranger had come, and he had gone - but the town, forever changed, would carry his lesson in its heart for generations to come.

CHAPTER TEN

The Easter Egg Hunt, Reborn

The first hints of spring began to stir in the air as the days grew longer and the snowdrops and crocuses poked through the damp earth of Maplewood. The town, still basking in the quiet glow of the transformation the mysterious stranger had left behind, found itself brimming with a different kind of energy this year. The streets were alive with the rustle of preparations, the sound of laughter, and the low hum of excited chatter as the townsfolk began to ready themselves for the annual Easter Egg Hunt.

But this year, there was something new. Something that could not be ignored, even by the most casual observer. It was as though the very essence of the town had shifted, its heart beating in a new, kinder rhythm, and it was impossible to miss. The Easter Egg Hunt, once a simple tradition, was now something more - a celebration of the lessons learned, a ritual of generosity, and a reflection of the change that had come to Maplewood.

Sophie and Henry stood at the edge of the square, watching as groups of children gathered, their faces bright with anticipation. There were the familiar faces - Lily, Max, and the others - but today they looked different. They looked... open. There was no boasting, no competitiveness in their eyes. Just the quiet understanding that had come from a year of reflection, a year of putting kindness above all else.

'This feels different, doesn't it?' Sophie asked, her voice quiet but full of wonder.

Henry nodded, his hands stuffed in his pockets as he surveyed the scene. 'It's like everyone's... happier. More together. I think the stranger's lesson really stuck. I know it stuck with me.'

Sophie smiled, her gaze drifting over the bustling square. Last year, the hunt had been a moment of revelation, a sharp, uncomfortable truth about the way appearances could be deceiving. But this year, the mood was different - lighter, gentler, and full of hope.

The tables in the square were lined with baskets, each one filled with eggs that, upon closer inspection, were strikingly different from those of the previous year. They weren't the glittering, eye-catching eggs of old, nor were they plain and unadorned. They were something else entirely - each one painted with care and love, decorated with flowers, swirls, and designs that seemed to capture the very spirit of kindness itself. They were not perfect, no, but they were real. Each egg had its own unique charm, its own story, and the children who gathered them would be choosing with their hearts, not with their eyes.

'I can't wait to see what's inside this year,' Henry said with a grin, kneeling down to examine one of the eggs in the basket. 'I hope they're filled with something nice.'

Sophie, her heart warm at the sight of the eggs, nodded. 'I think they will be. We've learned so much since last year, haven't we?'

Before Henry could answer, Lily and Max approached them, their eyes shining with the same excitement as the others. But there was no arrogance in their expressions now - only eagerness and a quiet humility that Sophie hadn't seen in them before. They had both changed, in ways that were subtle but unmistakable.

'Are you ready for the hunt?' Lily asked, her voice light, but there was a softness to it that made Sophie smile.

Max grinned. 'I think this year's going to be the best one yet. I'm excited to see what we find.'

'Me too,' Sophie replied, her heart swelling with gratitude. 'We've all learned something special, haven't we?'

Lily nodded, her eyes glinting with something deeper than the usual vanity. 'Yes. It's not about the eggs, is it? It's about what's inside.'

Sophie felt a flicker of joy at those words. Lily's transformation, though quiet and slow, was now undeniable. She had come to understand that true beauty - true value - was never on the outside. It was always, and forever, about what lay beneath the surface.

The town square was filling with more and more children, and the energy was palpable. The adults, too, were gathering, watching their children with quiet pride, the weight of last year's lesson carried in their hearts. The atmosphere was thick with the sense that this year's Easter Egg Hunt was going to be something special - something beyond a simple game.

As the clock struck ten, Mayor Thompson, who had once grumbled about the extravagance of the hunt, stepped to the front of the crowd, his voice booming in the now-silent square.

'Welcome, everyone, to the Maplewood Easter Egg Hunt!' he announced with a grin. 'This year, we've made a few changes. As you know, we've all learned a great deal from last year's hunt - from the lessons we learned and the lessons we've shared. This year, the eggs will be filled with something far more important than chocolate or candy. They'll be filled with the spirit of kindness, generosity, and the true beauty of the heart.'

A soft murmur of approval rippled through the crowd.

'Remember, this year, it's not the egg's appearance that matters - it's what's inside. And no matter what egg you find, you will find a gift. A gift of heart, a gift of kindness, a gift of care.'

There was a cheer from the children, their faces shining with excitement and anticipation.

'Now,' Mayor Thompson continued, 'go ahead! Find your eggs, but remember what really matters.'

The moment he finished, the children burst into action, their laughter ringing out like a chorus as they darted about the square, searching high and low for the eggs. Sophie, Henry, and their friends scattered in different directions, each child eager to discover what surprises lay inside the eggs they picked.

Sophie crouched down to pick up an egg that seemed rather plain at first glance. It was painted with gentle pastel colours - soft yellows and pinks - nothing that stood out. She cracked it open, curious, and to her delight, inside was a small, handwritten note. It read - *'True beauty lies in the kindness you share.'*

Her heart swelled, and she smiled as she tucked the note carefully into her pocket. It wasn't just the egg that mattered - it was the message. And this, she realised, was the real treasure.

Henry, just a few steps away, found an egg decorated with bright blue and green swirls. He opened it carefully and found a small packet of seeds, with a note attached: *'Plant kindness wherever you go.'*

He grinned and looked up to find Sophie. 'This is amazing. It's not just about us - it's about the whole town, isn't it?'

Sophie nodded, her eyes bright with understanding. 'It's about everyone.'

As the children continued to find their eggs, the square seemed to hum with a different energy. The eggs were filled with small acts of kindness - notes, seeds, poems, and little tokens of care that reminded everyone of what truly mattered. It wasn't just the hunt that was important. It was the joy in sharing, the joy in giving, the joy in understanding one another.

And as the sun began to dip low in the sky, casting a warm glow over the town, the feeling of togetherness was undeniable. The children, having completed their hunt, sat together in the square, exchanging their findings, their laughter filling the air as they shared their treasures with one another.

Maplewood was no longer just a town with a tradition. It was a town with a spirit - a spirit of kindness, generosity, and community. The stranger's lessons had taken root, and in their place, a new tradition had been born.

As Sophie and Henry walked home that evening, baskets light and hearts full, they looked out at the town of Maplewood - a town reborn, not by magic, but by the power of understanding, of kindness, and of the truth that what is inside is far more important than what is on the outside.

And in that moment, Sophie knew that this tradition, this lesson, would live on forever. For the Easter Egg Hunt, reborn, had become more than just a hunt. It had become a reminder - that true beauty is always found in the heart.

Epilogue

Years passed, as they always do, and Maplewood settled into its rhythm - quiet, familiar, and unchanged in many ways. But there was one thing that would never be the same. For the children who had once scrambled in the town square on that fateful Easter morning, there was a truth that lingered in their hearts, woven into the very fabric of who they had become.

Sophie, now a young woman with bright eyes and a gentle smile, walked along the cobbled streets of Maplewood with Henry by her side. The sun was setting, casting long shadows across the town, and the air was thick with the scent of blooming flowers and fresh grass. They passed by the old oak tree where they had once met as children, laughing and sharing stories, and where, for the first time, they had begun to understand what really mattered.

It was nearly Easter again, and as always, the town was preparing for the annual Easter Egg Hunt.

But this year was different. This year, it would not just be a celebration of the season - it would be a celebration of everything the town had become, thanks to the lessons of the past. The children who played in the streets, their laughter echoing through the air, no longer cared about appearances. They cared about kindness. They cared about generosity. And, above all, they cared about each other.

Sophie smiled to herself, remembering the stranger who had appeared all those years ago, his dark coat and wide-brimmed hat a mystery, his lessons a gift wrapped in silence. No one had ever truly understood where he had come from, or why he had chosen their town, but everyone had understood the lesson he left behind. It wasn't about the hunt. It wasn't about the eggs. It was about what lay within - the heart, the spirit, the soul.

And so, every year, as Easter approached, the eggs were filled with more than just sweet treats. They were filled with kindness. They were filled with little notes of encouragement, seeds to plant, tokens to remind the children of their true worth. It was a tradition that had been passed down, year after year, from child to child, from parent to child. And each year, the lesson grew stronger.

As Sophie and Henry reached the edge of the square, they noticed the familiar baskets waiting to be filled. There was Mrs. Wilkins, placing eggs with careful hands, and Mr. Jenkins, laughing with the children as they eagerly searched for their treasures. The eggs, now painted in vibrant colours and adorned with simple, yet beautiful designs, sparkled in the setting sun.

Sophie stopped, her heart swelling with gratitude. 'Do you ever wonder,' she asked Henry, 'if the stranger knew how much his lesson would change everything?'

Henry chuckled softly, his gaze softening as he looked at the scene around them. 'I think he knew. I think he knew it would take time, but the town would get it. And, in the end, the eggs were only a way to help us see what was always there.'

Sophie smiled, looking out across the square. The children were already beginning to gather, eager for the hunt, their faces alight with excitement. But there was something different about them - something that went deeper than their enthusiasm. They weren't just searching for eggs. They were searching for something more.

And that, Sophie thought, was the magic of it all.

As she and Henry made their way to the starting point, they could feel the warmth of the sun on their backs and the cool breeze in their hair, and they knew that the stranger, though gone, had left behind something far more powerful than any magic - he had left behind a town that truly understood the value of kindness.

The town of Maplewood had changed, and with it, so had the world.

And as the children of Maplewood eagerly began the hunt once more, Sophie couldn't help but think that, perhaps, the stranger's lesson wasn't just for the town. Perhaps, in the end, it was a lesson for all of them - the world, even.

True beauty, true worth, and true treasure - are never found in the things we see with our eyes. They are found in the hearts we touch, the kindness we give, and the love we share.

And that, Sophie knew, was the most magical thing of all.

As the first egg was found, the air was filled with the joyful laughter of children, echoing through the town, carrying the legacy of the stranger's lesson on the wings of time.

And Maplewood, forever changed, would carry it with them - always.

Printed in Great Britain
by Amazon